Where is she?

An Ivy and Mack story

Written by Deborah Friedland
Illustrated by Gustavo Mazali
with Adrienn Greta Schönberg

Collins

What's in this story?

Listen and say

river

path

Download the audio at www.collins.co.uk/839656

rain

sheep

field

grass

It was a beautiful spring day. Ivy and Mack went with Mum and Dad for a walk by the river.

4

There was a duck and lots of beautiful yellow flowers next to the water.

Ivy and Mack wanted to look in the river.
"I think there are some frogs in the water,"
said Mack. "And some baby frogs."

"You mean tadpoles!" said Ivy.

"Let's count the tadpoles!" said Mack.
"There are *lots* of them!" said Ivy.

Dad got some tadpoles. Mack counted them. "One – two – three – four – five – six – seven – eight – nine. Look, Dad! Ten tadpoles."

Mum saw a frog. "Look!" she said. "There's the tadpoles' mum!"

"I can't see her," said Mack. "Where is she?"

Mum pointed. "Right there! Look! Next to the duck."

"Yes! I can see her now," said Mack.

9

Dad looked at the sky. "Oh dear, rain," he said.

"It rains a lot in the spring," said Ivy.

"Yes," said Mum. "The flowers need the rain."

"Do the tadpoles get wet in the rain?" asked Mack.

Ivy laughed. "Tadpoles are *always* wet!"

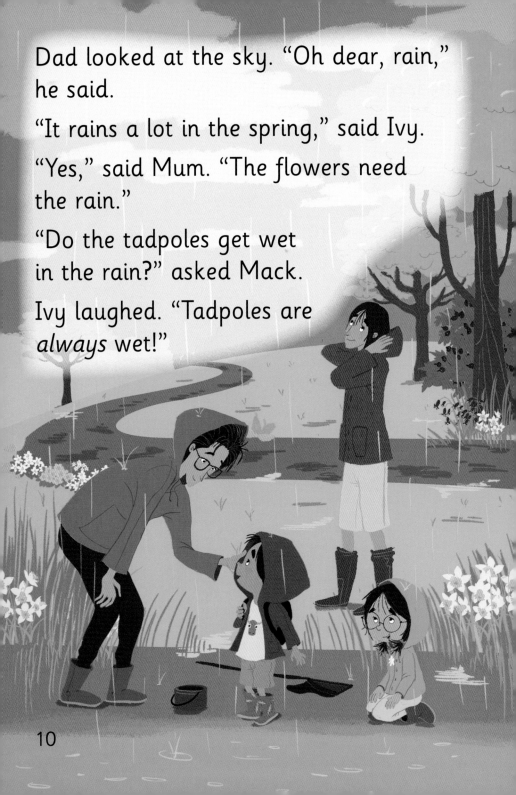

The rain stopped. "Let's go," said Dad. "Let's look at the sheep in this field."

"Look, Ivy! Mack! Can you see the lamb?" asked Mum.

They started to walk, but there was a lamb on the path.

"Hello, lamb," said Ivy and Mack.

"Where's your mummy?" Mack asked the lamb.

"Its mum isn't here," said Ivy.

"Where is she?" asked Mack.

"The lamb is crying!" said Ivy. "Dad, it wants its mother."

"Yes," said Mack. "Find its mother."

Dad looked at Mum. Mum looked at Dad.

"OK!" said Dad. "Come here, small lamb."

But it was difficult. The lamb ran from Dad.
"Quick, Dad!" said Ivy.
"It's there!" said Mack.
"In the yellow flowers!"

Dad came back with the lamb.
It was white and pretty.

Ivy and Mack loved the lamb.

"Now then, small one. We need to find your mum. Where is she?" said Dad to the lamb.

"Oh no! It's raining again," said Ivy. Mum, Dad, Ivy, Mack and the lamb stood under a tree. Dad looked into the field again. He saw a sheep with no lamb. The sheep looked at Dad.

Dad took the lamb to its mother.
The sheep was very happy.

"Hurray for Dad!" said Mack.

"Dad, you're so clever," said Ivy.

"Well done, Jay," said Mum.

Mum and Dad, Ivy and Mack finished their walk by the river. It was time to go home. "The grass is moving!" said Mack.

Mack looked at Ivy. "See those ducklings?" he said.

"Yes," said Ivy. "But their mother is not there. Where is she?"

"Oh, no!" said Dad. "Not again!"

Picture dictionary

Listen and repeat

duck

duckling

frog

lamb

sheep

spring

tadpole

1 Look and order the story

2 Listen and say

Collins

Published by Collins
An imprint of HarperCollins*Publishers*
Westerhill Road
Bishopbriggs
Glasgow
G64 2QT

HarperCollins*Publishers*
1st Floor, Watermarque Building
Ringsend Road
Dublin 4
Ireland

William Collins' dream of knowledge for all began with the publication of his first book in 1819.

A self-educated mill worker, he not only enriched millions of lives, but also founded a flourishing publishing house. Today, staying true to this spirit, Collins books are packed with inspiration, innovation and practical expertise. They place you at the centre of a world of possibility and give you exactly what you need to explore it.

© HarperCollins*Publishers* Limited 2020

10 9 8 7 6 5 4 3 2

ISBN 978-0-00-839656-5

Collins® and COBUILD® are registered trademarks of HarperCollins*Publishers* Limited

www.collins.co.uk/elt

British Library Cataloguing in Publication Data

A catalogue record for this publication is available from the British Library.

Author: Deborah Friedland
Lead illustrator: Gustavo Mazali (Beehive)
Copy illustrator: Adrienn Greta Schönberg (Beehive)
Series editor: Rebecca Adlard
Commissioning editor: Zoë Clarke
Publishing manager: Lisa Todd
Product managers: Jennifer Hall and Caroline Green
In-house editor: Alma Puts Keren
Project manager: Emily Hooton
Editor: Deborah Friedland
Proofreaders: Natalie Murray and Michael Lamb
Cover designer: Kevin Robbins
Typesetter: 2Hoots Publishing Services Ltd
Audio produced by id audio, London
Reading guide author: Julie Penn
Production controller: Rachel Weaver
Printed and bound by: GPS Group, Slovenia

MIX
Paper from
responsible sources
FSC™ C007454
www.fsc.org

This book is produced from independently certified FSC™ paper to ensure responsible forest management.

For more information visit: **www.harpercollins.co.uk/green**

Download the audio for this book and a reading guide for parents and teachers at www.collins.co.uk/839656